The TORTOISE and the HARE
AND OTHER STORIES

Contents

igloobooks

The Tortoise and the Hare

Once, there was a hare and a tortoise who were good friends, even though they were very different. Tortoise was **quiet** and liked to do things **slowly** and carefully. Hare was the opposite. He did things **quickly** and **boasted** about how fast he was.

"Let's have a race," said Tortoise, fed up of Hare's boasting.
"A race!" cried Hare. "Between a tortoise and a hare?"
"Yes," replied Tortoise. "Meet me on that hill tomorrow morning."
The other animals gasped. "I can't wait," said Hare, smiling.

The next morning, Hare and Tortoise met for the race. All their friends were there, too. **"Hare will definitely win,"** said Rabbit. **"I agree,"** said Field Mouse. **"Tortoise is so slow, he'll never keep up."** Hare warmed up by doing some press-ups and touching his toes. Tortoise just **stretched** out his little legs one at a time and then joined Hare, who was waiting at the starting line.

"READY, STEADY, GO!" shouted Crow.

Hare shot off down the track. **WHOOOOOSH!**

Tortoise plodded off, slowly and steadily, inching forward one step at a time.

Soon, there was a **huge** gap between Tortoise and Hare.
When Hare looked round, Tortoise was a long way behind him.
"This is so easy," thought Hare. **"I'm sure I'll win this race."**

Soon, Hare saw a patch of delicious dandelions. "I'll stop and eat," said Hare. "I'm **so far in front,** Tortoise will never catch up."

Hare ate and ate until he felt like he was going to **burst**. Moments later, he was fast asleep on the soft grass.

Far behind, Tortoise was plodding along. By the afternoon, he reached Hare. **"He must have stopped for a snack and fallen asleep,"** said Tortoise, chuckling.

Without a fuss, Tortoise moved steadily along, getting closer and closer to the finish line.

When Hare woke up it was evening time. Tortoise was just a speck, far ahead in the distance.

Hare **leapt** to his feet and **dashed** after Tortoise.

Flying overhead, Crow cheered him on.
"Come on, Hare!" he cawed.

Hare ran faster than he had ever run in his life. He got closer and closer to Tortoise. **"I'm going to win,"** he thought. However, as they crossed the finish line, Tortoise won by the length of a nose. From that day on, whenever he was tempted to boast, Hare remembered the day Tortoise had beaten him.

Slow and steady wins the race.

The Town Mouse
and the Country Mouse

Once, there were two mice who were cousins. One lived in the town. The other lived in the country. One day, Country Mouse invited his cousin to visit his home. Town Mouse arrived the very next day.

"You look very smart," said Country Mouse.

"Thank you," said Town Mouse.

After a short walk, Town Mouse's smart shoes were all **dirty**.

"In the town, I have clean pavements to walk on," he said.

"With boots like mine, you don't need clean pavements,"
replied Country Mouse.

At dinner, Town Mouse looked at his tiny plate of cheese and berries. He wrinkled his nose in dismay.
"Do you always eat such simple food?" he said.
"I don't need anything fancier," replied Country Mouse.

"You must come and visit me next time," said Town Mouse.
"I'll show you what you're missing."

Now it was Country Mouse's turn to visit his cousin in the town.
Once there, he looked up at Town Mouse's home in amazement.
"Your home is so very tall," said Country Mouse.
"It is rather wonderful, isn't it?" said Town Mouse, grandly.

Inside the house, it was so warm that Country Mouse had to take off his scarf and thick socks. **"This is a splendid house,"** he said.

Then, Town Mouse served enough food to feed a thousand mice. There were sandwiches, cakes and fruit, but **no cheese!**

"What a **magnificent feast**, cousin," said Country Mouse.
"**Please try everything,**" said Town Mouse. "Have **second helpings** if you wish."

Country Mouse had second, third and fourth helpings!
"**I think I could get used to living in the town,**" he said,
patting his stomach.

Suddenly, a giant cat strolled into the room. **"Aren't you going to invite me to join you?"** she purred. The two mice almost **jumped** out of their skin with fright.

Quick as a flash, they ran down the leg of the table...

... and **escaped** under the door

"**I miss my own home,**" said Country Mouse.

"**I understand,**" said Town Mouse. They shook paws and
waved goodbye to each other.

When he was back home, Country Mouse breathed in the fresh air.
"**This is the life for me,**" he said. "**Simple, quiet and no cats!**"

Better a little in safety, than an
abundance surrounded by danger.

The Fox and the Stork

The white stork was new to the pond. She had moved
into a nest nearby and wanted to meet her neighbours. She was
a very lovely, trusting bird and they liked her straight away.
"Welcome to our pond," said Heron and Flamingo.

"Morning, Fox."

"Hello, Fox."

Back at her nest, Stork realised Fox had played a **trick** on her. **"I shall have to teach him a lesson!"** she thought. So, the next time she saw Fox, she invited him round for dinner.

"I'd be delighted," said Fox, who mistakenly thought Stork had forgiven him.

Fox arrived for dinner. On the table were two tall jugs full of tasty soup. **"My nose won't fit in there,"** said Fox.
"Now you know how I felt," said Stork.
"I'm sorry," said Fox. **"I promise** I won't trick you ever again."

Always treat others as you
wish to be treated yourself.